Grammy's Hugs

Written by Barbara Adoff

Illustrations by Lucy He

For Iva,

Who taught me a kind of
Love I never imagined.

The first time I hugged you —
you were brand-spanking new.

My hug was so gentle,
you made the tiniest "cooo".

I promised myself on that very day
I would always hug you.
My hug was here to stay.

Hugging a baby is always a treat.
From the top of your head, to your pretend
"stinky feet".

Hugging a toddler is even more fun!
"Group Hug!" you would shout.
"All three, not just one."

Little Big Girl hugs are not hard to be found.
They come running right at you.
You end up on the ground!

Now our hugs had gone well, right up to this point.

But then you got older and said,
"I'm out of this joint!"

Off to Pre-School you went with friends
Asher and Sammy.
But the one you didn't expect to see there
was your huggable Grammy!

"What are you doing here at my school? Grammies can't be here! That is the rule."

So I explained how I promised
on that very first day.
I'd always be there to hug you,
no matter what people say.

Seeing that I was determined to stay,
you shrugged your shoulders and said:
"Well... Okay."

Pee Wee Soccer was fun! We'd run and run all day.
"Score!" we both shouted,
though we'd run the wrong way.

In third grade kids would ask,
`"What's that thing on your side?"
"Oh, that's just my Grammy. She refuses to hide."

So we went through grade school,
a slight pout on your lip.
I'd hug you all day as I sat at your hip.
Sometimes you'd have chocolate milk at lunch,
and give me a sip.

Middle School was a little more trying.

When a boy broke your heart we'd
both end up crying.

Ballet lessons paid off when you
danced in Swan Lake.
Your pliés were real. Mine were all fake.

When I hugged you at sleepovers
with all of your peers.
The girls would whisper and giggle.
You'd cover my ears.

You'd think it would be awkward,
me there in Senior High.
That the kids would make fun
and would want to know why.
But that didn't happen 'cause we had our hug pact.
They all understood. It was a matter of fact.

I felt kind of bad, and didn't want to be mean. But I think you got mad when I was voted Prom Queen.

You passed your driver's test and got your first car.
You went off to college; graduated a star.
You went for your first real job interview,
And through it all, I was right there with you.

Hugging and hugging with all of my heart.
So proud of my girl, so shiny and smart.

Time to fess up; for the truth to be told.

I was not really with you.

I would not be so bold.

But I kept my promise when we were apart.

My hugs were still with you.

They were hugs of the heart.

So my sweet grown-up little girl —
Make your own music and twirl your own twirl.
And always remember whether you see me or not,
I'll always be hugging you with all that I've got.

IvaBookForYou
www.ivabookforyou.com

Made in the USA
Coppell, TX
14 December 2021

68663499R10019